Mormon S

Brian Draper Tor

Our plan is supposed to happen tonight.

12:17:08PM

Pamela Lillian Valemont

ISBN: 978-1-326-41852-6

End of Days

It was a Friday at the end of August 2007, and two seventeen year old boys, Torey and Brian, sat next to each other chatting amicably in the back of the van on the three and a half hour ride from Pocatello to Kuna, located just outside Idaho's capital city of Boise. They hadn't seen each other in a while and had a bit of catching up to do.

As the drive continued, Brian Draper and Torey Adamcik talked about the things they shared: their upbringing in the Mormon Church and the event that occurred in their lives almost a year before, when they were both 16. They'd been hanging out together for only about six weeks, but the relationship had quickly escalated into one of close confidentiality, even to the exclusion of their usual company. It was a meeting of like minds. They were a pair met. Tight: like two fingers intertwined. They were able to share with each other thoughts that had been going around in their heads; things they could not discuss with any of their other friends, not even with their own families.

Fonnesbeck their driver, could overhear their conversation, and noted that it sounded a bit like a class reunion. They seemed to be at pains to reassure each other that they held no animosity toward each other for the past.

Who would have ever thought, they mused in wonder, that three days out of their lives would have such an enormous effect on them for the rest of their lives? They didn't mention specifically the culmination of that short interval of time, the date of September 22nd, nor the vitally significant event that erupted with volcanic force that day. Something they did that would cause them to spend the rest of their lives in prison.

They engaged in a little light-hearted banter with the driver. "We are just stupid kids. Can't you let us go?" they suggested to Lt. K.G. Fonnesbeck of the Bannock County Sheriff's Office. The flippant mood in the back waned somewhat when they saw the sign that caused their driver to turn off the freeway: Idaho Correctional Center. Soon the visually forbiddingly collection of drab brick buildings surrounded by high gun towers and reinforced steel compound wire, hove into view.

"You could sense they were getting a little more nervous. When you could see the yard, it got a little more real," related Fonnesbeck later.

Bad vibes: Pocatello, Idaho

Pocatello, Idaho, is a name that has a lasting connective memory for those involved in the hunt for serial killer, also a Mormon, Ted Bundy. A man who, shortly before his execution, confessed to 36 murders of girls and young women, one of whom was a 12 year old student at Alameda Junior High School in Pocatello. Bundy was subsequently captured in Pensacola, Florida, on 15th February, 1978, while on the prowl for yet another victim, long before Brian and Torey were even born.

The youths, born in 1990, were 16-year-old juniors at Pocatello High School when they committed an atrocious copycat murder. Their births came 15 years after the murder of the Pocatello Idaho schoolgirl, 12 years after Bundy's capture at Pensacola Florida and 9 years after Bundy's execution at Raiford Prison, Florida. Yet, I believe the known history of the horrific murder of a local 12 year old girl, abducted from a nearby junior high school, raped and murdered by the notorious necrophile and fellow Mormon Ted Bundy in their home town, had a profound affect upon these two young minds.

Their numerology charts reveal their vulnerability; their potential to develop violent tendencies in negative surroundings and the very great need for careful upbringing within a stable, moral, ethical and nurturing environment. Yet Torey reportedly owned 300 horror movies? What kind of sensible, caring parent with sound ethics, principles and morality allows that?

On the video tape they recorded prior to the crime, they can be seen and heard talking about serial killers and the very first name that comes out of their mouths is the name of Ted Bundy; how they wanted to emulate him and his horrific crimes. One can easily imagine how Bundy would be a hot topic of conversation among the high school youth of Pocatello, given the fact that he had murdered one of their female school children. They too, wanted to

4

earn a notorious reputation exactly like his. He was their hero. Anti-hero to be exact.

But how did they figure that along with such notoriety would not go a life prison sentence? Bundy died in the electric chair on 24th January, 1989, the very year their victim was born. They must have known that. Why then, did they think that the crime they were about to commit would not come with like consequences? It seems that both boys were incapable of basic logical reasoning. Neither mentioned the risk they were about to take; of being caught and incarcerated for their crimes.

They were able to justify their total lack of moral conscience over the planned murder of their schoolfriend, a girl the same age as themselves, by saying it was part of their plan and that nothing could interfere with that plan. They were quite obsessive about it. They had all their ducks in a row. Cassie, their intended victim was, they said, "perfect" for the crime. Perfect – how? Long, dark hair, parted in the middle: exactly the way almost every one of Ted Bundy's victims wore their hair? Coincidence, or design? Too bad about her family, they reckoned. They showed token sympathy for them, none at all for the young girl whose life they were planning to take. Every word, every action appertaining to this proposed murder, and the later carrying out of it, recorded on tape for posterity to witness, exposes the pair as textbook young psychopaths, aka sociopaths.

Her body was never found

Pocatello is the largest city in Bannock County, straddling neighbouring Power County, where a small portion of the city spreads onto the Fort Hall Indian Reservation, in the US state of Idaho. Snake River winds its way alongside the reservation. On the 6th of May, 1975, Ted Bundy's plan was laid. He had a room at the Pocatello Holiday Inn, booked for the express purpose of killing a young girl. Any young girl. He had yet to find her.

12 year old Lynette Culver was on her lunch break from Alameda Junior High School, (located on Alameda Road, some 20 minutes driving distance from the Horizon Inn), when Bundy approached her. He may have lured Lynette into his vehicle with charm and

guile, or after their initial conversation, he may have coerced her and forced her to cooperate, as he did with his final victim Kimberly Leach, another 12 year old girl he murdered in Florida.

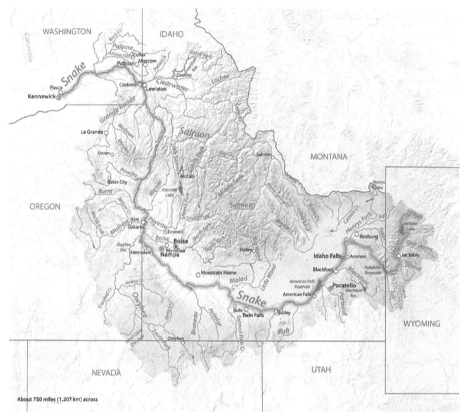

Path of the Snake River, winding its way past Pocatello, rounding the Fort Hall Indian Reservation before running into the American Falls Reservoir. Boise can also be seen on the map. Nearby Kuna is the location of the Idaho Correctional Center, where Corey and Brian are now incarcerated.

Whatever the case, her killer learned of certain details about Lynette only she could have provided to him. Prior to the short walk from his prison cell down the corridor to Old Sparky, at Raiford Prison in Starkey Florida, detectives listened to what Bundy had to tell about Lynette, as part of his deathbed confessions.

"She made a comment that sounded like she had other friends or relatives in Seattle…Made a comment indicating that she either lived with her grandmother or that her grandmother lived with her family. Another comment indicating that perhaps they were thinking of moving to another house. Indications that she had had some trouble with truancies at school…and…finally that I encountered her at a time when she was leaving the school grounds to meet someone at lunch time."

Number **29** indicates the whereabouts of the Holiday Inn. Insert: 12 year old Lynette Culver, victim of Ted Bundy, typical in appearance in that she had long dark hair parted up the middle, as did Cassie Stoddart.

He related how he took her back to the Pocatello Holiday Inn located at **1399** Bench Road.

$$1399 = 1+3+9+9 = \text{Master 22} = \begin{array}{cccc} R & A & P & E \\ 9 & 1 & 7 & 5 \end{array}$$
$$= \text{Master 22}$$

He did not say if she went willingly to the hotel or if he knocked her out prior to taking her there, which was his usual MO. He drowned her in the bath tub and had sex with her dead body. He did not say if she was taking a bath at will at the time he killed her, or if he knocked her out and then filled the bath with water solely for the purpose of drowning her in it. We can take an educated guess that the latter (mercifully) applied, since Bundy's admitted prime sexual motivation, the driving force behind his heinous crimes, was necrophilia.

He then carried her to out of the unit and put her body in his car, standing at the ready right by the back door, and drove to the Snake River, where he threw her body into the water. When questioned why he had killed Lynette, sexually interfered with her dead body, and dumped her in the river, he calmly lifted his bowed head, made eye contact and said, "It was the madness." Bundy was very good at blaming "the entity" inside him. Brian and Torey, on the other hand, had each other to blame.

Brian and Torey blame each other in separate trials

Prior to the pleasant conversation exchanged on their ride to prison, the pair faced trials where they attempted to blame each other for the crime, absolving themselves of responsibility.

Torey Adamcik and Brian Draper could have requested separate cars or a barrier to separate them in the Bannock County sheriff's van during the ride to the Idaho State Correction Institution. Instead, they elected to sit next to each other and chat. Perhaps at their tender age, they needed to shore each other up somewhat?

Draper and Adamcik were convicted in separate trials of first-degree murder and conspiracy to commit first-degree murder in the slaying of 16-year-old Cassie Jo Stoddart. They were arrested on 27th September 2006; five days after Cassie Stoddart was attacked and stabbed at least 29 times while petsitting for relatives in northeast Bannock County. Though Cassie was not raped, it is clear from the recording made by the boys immediately prior to the crime, that there was a sexual motive. Corey mentions he has a hard on just thinking about knifing Cassie to death.

The Pythagorean Life Theorem
"A Blueprint for Your Life"

Birth Name: Torey Michael Adamcik
Birthdate: 14th June, 1990= 39/3 Spirit Force or Life Lesson

TOR+6= 20+15+18+6 = <u>59/5</u>
EYM+14 = 5+25+13+ 14 = 57/3
ICH+1990=9+3+8+(1990=19) = 39/3

Personal Year at time of Cassie Jo Stoddart's murder: 14+6+2006
last birthday = 28/1 Personal Year, + 9th month = 37/1 Personal
Month, + 22nd day = <u>59/5</u> Personal Day

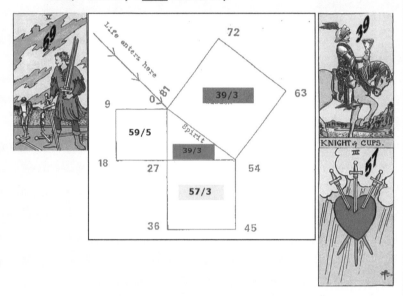

Bannock County Sheriff Detention Centre

Significance of the Number 59 appearing on Torey's chart twice

The **Number 59** appearing on Torey's birth chart and showing as the number vibration he was functioning under on the day of the murder, indicates he is guilty as hell, despite his protestations of innocence. He was no innocent bystander. The **Number 59** indicates the possibility of his being

either (a) the perpetrator

or (b) the victim of this type of crime.

It is a number particularly relating to a serial killer **or a serial killer in the making,** and this crime fits exactly that mould.

Victim Kimberly leaves clue behind identifying killer Ted Bundy - the Number 59

I would like to now insert here an excerpt from my book on serial killer Ted Bundy, which highlights the negative affects of this grim number, 59.

Just as Bundy left numerological clues behind, so too did his victims. We have seen and read futuristic detective crime movies and novels where the last visual image the victim has seen while alive is permanently etched, mirrored in the retinas of the dead. Detectives of the future are able to reproduce this photographic image then broadcast it all over the media, making the tracking and identification of the killer a comparatively easy task. Well, I have always thought that if you can visualize an invention, it will happen one day. Certainly, I have visualized a few that have now eventuated. But we may be centuries away from that kind of assistance in finding killers.

But right here, right now, there are clues that the dead leave behind that will help us connect to the killer. I have not been able to obtain many dates of birth and full names of Bundy's victims, only those of Melissa Smith, Margaret Bowman, and Kimberly Leach, from pictures of headstones recorded on the Internet. The pattern is not the same in each victim, but they are correlations with numbers on

Bundy's chart in each case. It may be that the ruse, that is the method used in snatching the victims varied, and consequently the clues change.

```
THEODORE   ROBERT    C O W E L L
45              Master 33   3 6 5 5 3 3
=45             33          =25
=       103 =4 Destiny
Master 44/8 Soul
        59/5 Personality Projection to the world


TED COWELL
11   25
   = 36/9 Destiny
      16/7 Soul
      20/2 Personality

 THEODORE   ROBERT   NELSON
45              33          5 5 3 1  6 5
=   45          33          = 25
= 103 = 4 Destiny
   44/8 Master Soul
   59/5 Personality


TED NELSON
11   25
   = 36/9 Destiny
      16/7 Soul
      20/2 Personality
```

I don't doubt that Bundy could sense the type of vulnerability of each victim, much as a dog smells a bone in the next yard, goes over and steals it. In other words, he operated at the animalistic, instinctive level. He would have exploited the distinct kind of vulnerability of each of his victims. Separating the victim from those who might protect her, isolating her and thus making her prone to attack, is central to his modus operandi.

It may also be that his reason for taking each particular victim varied too, and the type of crime committed will reflect this. Although on the surface it seemed Bundy killed for the same reasons, we may be assuming too much there. Perhaps he had, as he thought anyway, different reasons for selecting each of his victims, and not only his initial approach but also his treatment in dealing with each of them would have been different. Bundy always maintained his victims were nothing alike, though onlookers could see a distinct similarity in appearance. All had long, dark hair, parted in the middle.

I immediately noticed a clue in the case of 12-year-old Kimberly Leach, the conviction of whose murder put Bundy in the electric chair. This connection with the Number 59 I was to find repeated again and again in some way with every case of murder and serial murder I researched.

Twelve year old Kimberly, a native of Scorpio, who was born on October 28th 1965 = 59/5, and whose DNA led to the conviction of serial killer Ted Bundy and inexorably to his execution in the Florida electric chair. A grim reminder of the tragedy and heartbreak Bundy left in his wake. The grave of 12 year old Kimberly Dianne Leach whose body Bundy left in a deserted pigsty. He went to the electric chair for this heartless, heinous crime.

✓ **Kimberly**, born on October 28th, 1965, had a **59/5** Life Lesson/Spirit Force Number; that is, her date of birth adds up to 59/5: 28+10+ ((1965=1+9+6+5) =21)) = **59/5**.

- ✓ **Bundy** was in a **Personal Year** having a vibration of the **Number 59/5** when he killed her. **Bundy in a Personal Year having a vibration of the number 59/5, running from 24/11/1977- 24/11/1978.** His last birthday before the murder fell on 24th November, 1977 = 24+11+(1+9+7+7=24)= **59/5**

- ✓ **Bundy's Personality Number** at birth was the **Number 59/5**, that is the value of the consonants in the birth name of Theodore Robert Cowell. It was also the Personality Number of the name his mother bestowed upon him later, before she married Ted Bundy – Theodore Robert Nelson.

```
S E R I A L   K I L L E R
1 5 9 9 1 3   2 9 3 3 5 9
=28          + 31
```
- ✓ = 59/5   **This term was coined for Ted Bundy**, when detectives in several states, by looking at the similar nature of the crimes, realized they were all searching for the same man.

It was Kimberly Dianne Leach, with a Life Lesson of the Number 59/5, whose DNA convicted Ted Bundy and sent him to the electric chair. She was the last in a long line of what police believe was perhaps hundreds of victims. In similar fashion, Allison Baden-Clay, who had acquired the Destiny Number of the **Number 59/5** on her marriage to Gerard through the change in surname upon marriage, became the person whose frantic scratches left tell-tale marks upon his face, and convicted him in no uncertain manner of her murder. As such, it is clear that the Number 59/5, while it rules death and burial, **also rules forensic evidence that convicts the killer.** The video tape and knives that Corey and Brian buried held the forensic evidence that securely put them behind bars, interminably.

The Number 59 is the most telling number on Bundy's chart, one that directly connects him to the kinds of crimes committed. The Number 59 rules abduction on the highway, masses and rites said over the body of the dead, and burial. I believe Bundy's motive for this particular crime was necrophilia.

The **Five of Swords** equating with the **Number 59**

Perhaps in Bundy's warped, twisted mind, the abandoned farrowing shed constituted some sort of burial tomb. The Five of Swords is the pictorial image for the **Number 59**. Note the highway on which the figure stands. The **Number 59** also rules capture of the perpetrator by means of forensic evidence left at the scene of the crime. Fibres and hairs found in the stolen van used to abduct, rape and murder Kimberly provided the means to convict Bundy and send him to the electric chair.

I was also able to establish that Ted Bundy had been in a **59/5** Personal Month when he murdered 8 year old Ann Marie Burr, in his home town of Tacoma, when he was only 14 years old. Ann lived just a few streets away from Ted and knew him from his paper route he did in the area. She was abducted from her home in the middle of the night.

Likewise, he was in a **Personal 59/5** Year when he committed the two murders at the Chi Omega sorority house, the maiming for life of other victims at that address and the attack at Dunwoody Street, which left a ballet dancer of great potential with a pronounced limp, unable to pursue her dreams of becoming a ballerina. All of these attacks occurred on the same night. Yet, look at his defiantly swaggering stance below, as the triple murder indictment for the deaths of Margaret Bowman, Lisa Levy and Kimberly Leach is read out to him.

Bundy at press conference in Tallahassee announcing his triple murder indictment, July 1978 (State Archives of Florida).

Murder on February 9th 1978, of Kimberly Dianne Leach (aged 12): Abducted from her junior high school in Lake City, Florida; skeletal remains found near Suwannee River State Park. The next day Bundy backtracked 60 miles (97 km) westward to Lake City. At Lake City Junior High School that morning, 12-year-old Kimberly Diane Leach was summoned to her homeroom by a teacher to retrieve a forgotten purse; she never returned to class. After an intensive search, her partially mummified remains were found seven weeks later in a pig farrowing shed near Suwannee River State Park, 30 miles (48 km) from Lake City.

She was clearly vulnerable to attack by the likes of Bundy. Had this little girl been made more aware of not believing anything a stranger tells her, of never going away with a stranger before first checking with someone she knows that it's OK to do so, she would be alive today. Several people saw a distressed, crying child being forcibly led away by an angry young man, yet none intervened. None even reported the fact to the police. They only came forward later when it was known what had happened to the young girl; after her body was found four months later.

We must try ever to uplift and better humanity; strive for the higher good, the higher purpose in life. We must never take things lying down; think we can never eradicate the evil in the world. Refusal to accept evil is the reason why this world has progressed and evolved into something better than it was hundreds of years ago; we are now on a higher spiritual plane because of the insistence of billions of people generationally that we must do better, aim ever higher.

In regard to the murder under discussion, this description above, notes "a critical moment in life" and also the man who is head of the operation, that is, "master of the field." Waite also draws attention to the necessity for discipline of children.

I must state right here and now that I reject out of hand any suggestion that Kimberly's and Cassie's fate was "karmic". That kind of talk is very dangerous. We cannot give the perpetrators of such hideous crimes any excuse at all. There is no justification on this earth for the evil crimes of the likes of Bundy, Draper or Adamcik. The latter two state on their video that they had tried several times to kill someone, but their plan always had to be put on hold because of some impediment. They did have plans to kill more and more people. If they had gotten away with their crime, they may well have gone on to do that.

Karma to me is, simply put, very sad or very glad news coming into the life. We have no idea what the reason for this is, God alone knows that. It is not up to us to conjecture on such things. We are only human, not divine. I do not believe in "bad karma" and a system put in place to punish even the innocent newborn for their past bad deeds in a former life; that is by retribution for same. People who believe they know such things are among those who insist people with cancer have a death wish, that they do not really want to get well - it must be their fault if they die.

Such people are cruel and heartless; moreover they have no vision at all. They are stunted in their spiritual growth, and they stunt the world by believing that way. If we are to encompass such beliefs, we might as well give up on a future for humanity.

For all we know, it may be that the victims of such cruel crimes are such outstanding people they must suffer in order to make criminals pay for their crimes. That is one possibility I will allow, but it is by no means proven, nor will it ever be. We may one day find out about the heavenly order of things - when we leave this earth and journey to the next one - even then our finding out anything at all about A Divine Plan is by no means guaranteed. It is something we might hope for. That's about the extent of it, in my opinion.

Traditional meaning of the Five of Swords: Loss, dishonour, degradation, defeat, ruin, reversal of fortune, diminution, wronging, bad luck, destruction, etc. Reversed: Much the same, burial, obsequies. It is also said to represent a thief and theft, corruption, seduction, plague, and all that is hideous and horrible.

The element of Earth with its influence of Mars and Saturn on the Fifth house, ruling the heart, cannot be very 'favourable' in the ordinary sense of the word and is certain to lead to a feeling of being wronged by the world, an inner bitterness and impotence, which hinders enterprise and business; so these will suffer.

And the heart itself, being of precisely the opposite nature, will suffer and find things awkward, horrible, hideous, etc. In the same way this card must indicate affliction of honour, which is ruled by the Sun. Moreover, as "from the heart are the issues of life," the card may indicate vice and a bad use of the inner or spiritual forces. Still there is another possibility, and this is given by Mr. Waite when he says that this card's image signifies a man who "is master of the field." So he may be if the inner force is great enough to conquer the afflictions which assail him.

In other words, it need not be a card of absolute defeat, for there may very well be a good result, but nevertheless it denotes serious difficulty and **a critical moment or period in life**, in which the person so affected or some one to whom that person relates will be threatened with the above-mentioned sad effects.

CONCLUSION: Affliction, crisis, morose disposition, bitterness, impotence, lack of self-respect, or self-confidence; it may be that self-confidence is ascertained by some struggle or conflict;

difficulties, which after all may prove very useful but necessitate much self-discipline. In the same way discipline of children is necessary. General Book of the Tarot, by A. E. Thierens, [1930]

Cycle: from his birthday on 14th June to 14th October, 2006, Torey was in a four-month-cycle ruled by his age at the time, 16. He helped to murder Cassie during that period of time, on 22nd September, 2006.

2006 last birthday before the murder
   16+ age he was at the time
20**22**= **6** Cycle, mediated through the Master 22.
The Murder occurred on the 22nd.

T O R E Y   M I C H A E L A D A M C I K
2 6 9 5 7   4 9 3 8 1 5 3 1 4 1 4 3 9 2
= Master 29 Master 33   24
86= 14/5 Destiny
Master 44/8 / 37/1 Dual Soul
42/6 / 49/4 Dual Personality

Torey   Adamcik
Master 29 24
 = 53/8 Destiny
   Master 22/4 / Master 29/11 Dual Soul
   31/4/ 24/6 Dual Personality

S T A B B I N G R A P E
1 2 1 2 2 9 5 7 9 1 7 5
= Master 29/11   = Master 22/4

M I L I T A R Y P R I S O N
4 9 3 9 2 1 9 7 7 9 9 1 6 5
= Master 44/8   = 37/1

Draper and Adamcik, when they turned 17, were transferred from Bannock Juvenile Detention Center to an adult prison at Kuna, near Boise, Idaho. After their arrival at the prison which was to be their final destination, they were held in the reception and diagnostic unit to be evaluated.

"It takes two to four weeks to evaluate new inmates," said Jeff Ray, a department spokesman. "They undergo psychological evaluations, physical evaluations, and their educational needs are assessed." That process was designed to determine where they would be placed in the Idaho Department of Correction's system. Inmates who are considered vulnerable are segregated from the rest of the prison population for their safety.

```
B R I A N    L E E    D R A P E R
2 9 9 1 5   3 5 5   4 9 1 7 5 9
= 26          13           35
= Master 74/11 Destiny
         26/8 Soul
         48/3 Personality
```

Brian Draper
26   35
= 61/7 Destiny
  16/7 Soul
  45/9 Personality

THE TOWER.

The Number 16 has historical connections with the infamous Tower of London, and in modern times, with the country of America and the terrorist attacks on the Twin Towers.

Brian Lee Draper was born on the 21st March, 1990. That makes him an Arian, and I am not at all surprised. He looks like one, but he is born right on the cusp of Pisces, which leaves him straddling both signs. It is highly unusual to find any Piscean involved in such a cruel crime. Con artists they can be, but murderers? Never. Arians, on the other hand, can very well manifest cruel traits, as Aries is symbolically the God of War. Adolf Hitler was an Arian, thought right on the cusp of Taurus, at the other end of the month, 20th April. Taurus the Bull can also be cruel. The gentle Piscean Fish is not usually known for cruelty at all. Deceptive they may be, but they are not normally cruel people.

I thank Bonnie Kernene sincerely for providing Brian's date of birth for me to analyse. This information was vital if I was to complete this book properly. I had written to Brian himself, also his mother, but they had not replied; so, had Bonnie not contacted me, this book could not have been finished in full. I would have been able to tell only half the story.

Brian Lee Draper born on the 21st March, 1990= 43/7 Life Lesson.

BRI+3= 2+18+9+3= 32/5
ANL+21= 1+14+12+21= 48/3
EEB+1990=5+5+2+19=31/4

22nd September 2006 date of the murder.
Brian's last birthday before the attack on Cassie fell on 21st March, 2006: 21+3+2006= 32/5

So, Brian was in a 32/5 Personal Year at the time of Cassie's murder

He was in a 41/5 Personal Month – ruling mutilation of body, (usually this means surgery with a scalpel) and there is a connection with the heart centre. Brian, I believe, stabled Cassie through the heart. This may also indicate a case of unrequited love.

The Number 5 rules the heart centre on the human body. The heart is a living organ that supplies blood to every part of the human body. When it ceases pumping, the body dies. When a human being stands with arms and legs outstretched, there are 4 points on the compass of the human body. The head is the 5th point, but it relies on the crucial heart centre to supply it with blood or it will die. The brain and the heart are inextricably connected, and so the heart was regarded as the 5th point on the human compass by the ancients, who believed that the heart was the focus of all human emotions. We are now coming to recognize that this is indeed true: grief can kill and shock can kill people too, by causing the heart to fail in certain extremely traumatic situations. The possibility also exists that Cassie may have died of shock and grief during the attack, that her heart may have failed and ceased to beat; but of course, the equally strong likelihood exists that a stab through the heart killed her.

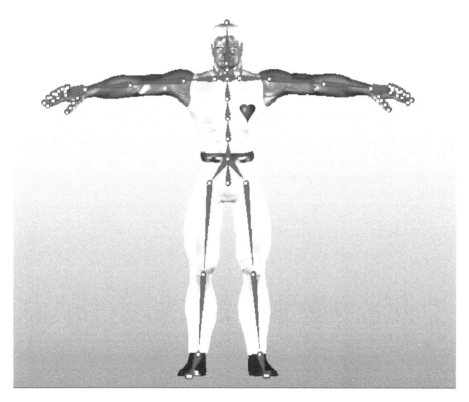

Brian was in either a 62/8 or a 63/9 Personal Day, depending on his time of birth. 41+22nd day = 63/9 Personal Day = Lord of Cruelty. If his time of birth was prior to the time the attack on Cassie commenced, then he was in his 22nd day already, and therefore functioning under the 63/9 vibration. We do not know Brian's time of birth because he was adopted, but I think it is safe to say he was in his Personal 63/9 day at the time he participated in the murder of Cassie.

It is interesting to note that at the time he videotaped Cassie at school, when she was putting her books away in her locker, he would in all likelihood have been transiting his 62/8 Personal Day equating with the 8 of Swords and this symbolism is quite frightening when you consider that this number concerns a woman who cannot see what is going on, yet is treading a very dangerous path. She is surrounded by a cage of swords, (knives) but is (symbolically) blindfolded and cannot see them. Although she may not be entirely oblivious to what is around her, she fails to act on her basic instincts. Cassie had no idea of Brian's intention of being a party to her murder as he casually interviewed her, mentioning Corey, his intended co-conspirator, by name.

However, she may have felt uneasy and a trifle embarrassed about the attention she was getting, but failed to act on her subconscious suspicions. She did in fact, allow Brian and Torey to visit her and Matt on the night she was killed. It appears she may even have invited them over. She virtually unwittingly opened the door to her killers and invited them in. She may have known full well that both boys were attracted to her, but felt safe and secure in the company of her boyfriend Matt. She did not perceive either boy as being a threat to her or to Matt, which they clearly were. She was oblivious to the danger surrounding her.

This card also concerns someone who does not voice, or is prevented from voicing, his intentions or speaking his mind. He is suppressed by rules and regulations and governing bodies or authorities. Brain (and Torey) were worried that a female teacher was watching them while they planned and plotted the murder, videotaping their intentions, with Torey writing the whole thing down on paper for posterity. This piece of paper was a key piece of evidence that would put both of them away for life. All of these things concerning restriction for the perpetrators and the victim being unaware of what is approaching her applied in this situation, and this is graphically depicted on the Tarot Card symbolism for the Number 62.

The Number 62 is followed by the Number 63, and this card, the Nine of Swords, known as The Lord of Cruelty, graphically depicts the lamentations and suffering of Cassie, as she lies in her bed of pain, surrounded by the swords (knives) that engulf her. The quilt on her bed symbolises the painful experiences life has brought her. Her final thoughts must have been ones of horrible realization of the naïve trust she placed in the murderers she thought were her friends, Brian and Torey. Cassie, lying grotesquely on the living room floor in a pool of blood, was found by a young female relative on the family's return from a short vacation.

This card may also depict the sorrow and suffering Brian now faces because of his actions on the day of Cassie's murder. Locked in a small cell, he has nothing much in there at all, except a bed to lie on. At night, lying in his bed, he is surrounded by nothing but horrible recollections of what he did to Cassie, by extension to her family, and what he has done to his own family who love him. Nothing but painful regrets for the rest of his life. Brian's parents have moved to be near him, and continue to support him through what will be the long, interminable years of imprisonment.

```
T O R E Y        S T A B B I N G
2 6  9  5 7      1 2  1  2 2  9 5 7
= Master 29/11   = Master 29/11
```

To give an example of the way the Number 41/5 rules the heart centre negatively, here is an analysis of the words, "coronary occlusion".

```
C O R O N A R Y   O C C L U S I O N
3 6 9 6 5 1 9 7   6 3 3 3 3 1 9 6 5
= 85= 13/4 = Death Card- (Roman Numerals XIII) aggregate
   44/8 Master Value of the vowels
   41/5 Value of the consonants
```

Cycle Brian was in at the time of the murder: this cycle, was ruled by his Life Lesson of 43/7 and ran from 21st July to 21st November, 2006

2006 last birthday
   43+Life Lesson
2049= 15/6 Cycle

A **15/6 Cycle**, mediated through the **Number 49/4.**

The **Number 15** (Roman Numerals XV) equates with **The Devil Card** and the **Number 6** with **The Lovers Card**, (Roman Numerals VI).

THE DEVIL . | THE LOVERS. | DEATH .

Time does not heal all wounds

It's September 2015, at time of writing. Ten years since Cassie Jo Stoddart was murdered by two male school friends in her Aunty Allison's and Uncle Frank's house at Tyhee, Idaho. Cassie and her killers were all 16 years old back then, when the murder that scattered terror like shrapnel through the neighbourhood took place. It engendered fear and shattered lives of those most affected by the wake of its blast. Her killers have grown older, but Cassie's photo shows her frozen in time: she will always be 16.

Brian and Torey are now 25 years old, firmly locked up in an adult prison 231 miles away from the scene of that incredibly heartless, viciously cold blooded attack. No vestige of evidence of their insanely demented attack is apparent on their visages. Tears fall, but are they of genuine remorse, or self-pity? In Brian's case, he appears genuinely contrite, deeply ashamed and truly sorry for the attack. Perhaps he is capable of rehabilitation? He says Torey is virtually stifled and stymied because he still has been unable to confess to his part in the crime. This could well be the fault of his parents, who are terrified he will confess, and they will have to face the horrible truth of what their son has done.

A decade later, the shock has abated but the aftermath of pain has not gone away. Memories haunt the home and remain firmly entrenched in the minds of those who live there, as well as those in the local area and wider vicinity. So much so, that Cassie's relatives are unable to sell their home and move on. In the same way that many refuse to believe the two youthful killers are now steeped in sorrow, nobody will buy it. Who can blame them?

Any newcomers to the area are inevitably informed of the tragic history of the lovely split level house set high in the pretty country surrounds on Whispering Cliffs Drive. The name has taken on ominous overtones. There are said to be ghostly whispers inhabiting the walls, an eerie presence permeates the living room where the murder took place. Invariably, potential buyers are frightened off. And it has become a home depicted in a real life horror film for those who dwell within its confines. They too, have been sent to prison, yet not one of their own devising and making.

Family tragedy has a way of splitting apart and rendering inharmonious what under normal circumstances would be happy, united homes. In 2005, Frank and Allison Contreras and their blended brood of three were excited about their move from the Bay Area of California to the peaceful tranquillity of a two acre country property in Idaho.

They did not have long to enjoy their dream home and the relaxed, pleasant country life it afforded. Surrounded by soothing names like Moonglow Lane, White Cloud Drive, and Sage Hollow, reminiscent of the peace and love flower power hippy era, the family felt protected and safe from harm. There was no hint of the shadow that would fall across their world and put it out of the sunlight and into the shade.

Just a year later, their dream home became a filmic Nightmare on Whispering Cliffs Drive. It was inside Frank and Allison's contented family home that Cassie Jo, Frank's lovely young niece with the long dark hair, parted in the middle, was stabbed to death by her classmates, Torey and Brian.

The killing was callously, coldly planned, enacted in a sexually excited frenzy, brutally, violently carried out. A thrill kill: Cassie was stabbed at least 29 times; taken unawares, while she was pet and house-sitting for Frank and Allison. Her frenemies, Torey and Brian, had visited with Cassie and her boyfriend Matt earlier in the evening before contriving to leave for home. Matt too was an intended victim, but their plan was thwarted by Matt's parents coming to collect him. Cassie, left alone in the home, became the sole target.

Cassie Jo Stoddart

"Cassie was a good girl," Frank said. "She didn't drink or use drugs and she was a straight A student. She was responsible. We didn't just trust her with our house, she babysat my son too."

Cassie was killed on Friday night. Allison's 13-year-old daughter, Frank's step-daughter, found Cassie lying dead on the living room floor when the family returned home Sunday evening. The young girl suffered a breakdown after finding Cassie's body and later attempted suicide. Frank said each member of the family has had an unexplained encounter in the home.

The local community rallied around the Contreras family in the wake of the terrible crime and the grief that naturally accompanies such an occurrence. The Bannock County Sheriff's Office put them all up in a hotel for two weeks during the murder investigation, and Sheriff Lorin Nielsen helped fund the insurance pay out to expedite the clean up process, in readiness for their return.

Despite the fact that the house has now been freshly painted, and there's a new carpet in the spacious living room, the scene of the crime, it's a ghost room because "We just never went back in there," Frank said.

On this particular day, while the rest of the cemetery is bathed in sunlight, a shadow falls over the grave of Cassie Jo Stoddart, as though signalling from beyond that the manner of her death has been judged especially heinous.

The bad-vibe white-elephant room cannot be extracted like a tooth from the rest of the house, and that empty, unused room exuding its all consuming sadness impacted on Frank's entire family. His wife Allison became clinically depressed and as a result of being unable to work, lost her job.

Frank had to work two jobs to keep the home afloat. "Medication alone was $300 a month," Frank said. "The first two years were the worst. It was our dream home, and it turned into a nightmare." Under other circumstances, the house would have any real estate agent rubbing his hands together with glee at the prospect of selling it for clients. The well constructed and attractively designed house sits on two acres off Two and a Half Mile Road and features 1,600-square feet of family space, fenced pastures and a garage. But it no longer feels like home and it hasn't since 22nd September, 2006.

Pocatello Realtor Randy Spencer knows he has an unrealistic challenge ahead of him, an enormous barrier to hurdle. At the outset, he is not obligated to disclose to potential buyers that a violent murder took place at the property they are inspecting. But once that prospective buyer becomes a committed client, at the point at which a contract is drawn up for signature, the realtor must by law divulge the unwelcome information.

Frank Contreras, Uncle Frank to victim Cassie Jo Stoddart.

After criminal conviction at trial, the appeals process inevitably ensues. It's a normal part of due process. But every fresh appeal renews afresh the horrific manner in which Cassie died. "I just quit loving and started drinking," said Frank. "It put pressure on my marriage and my family." Allison still lives in the house with their 12-year-old son, but Frank no longer lives there.

11372 W Whispering Cliffs Drive, Pocatello.

Frank said the family is doing much better — he's doing much better — but they feel trapped in a house that won't sell; one they can no longer stand to live in. "We just want out, but we want to fulfil our financial obligation." Frank said. "We're at the point that we will take what we owe: $138,000. We just want to walk. But there is this stigma on this house." A decade down the track, there are still no buyers, not even at fire sale price. It is safe to assume that property values for others living in close proximity would have plummeted in the wake of the murder as well. Like a stone dropped in a lake, the ripples have extended further and further around the house of undeserved ignominity, encompassing all in the surrounding area.

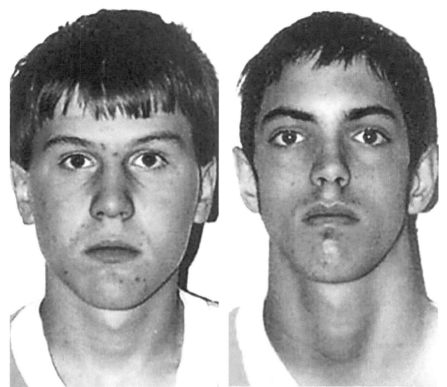

Torey Adamcik left and Brian Draper right at the time of their crime

8:10:43PM
SEP 21 2006

There should be no law against killing people. I know it's a wrong thing but... hell...

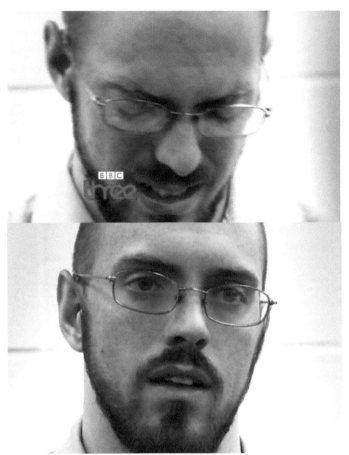

Brian Draper today

Torey Adamcik

Torey Adamcik speaks to his father

Anna Stoddart, centre, mother of Cassie Jo.

The back and front of Cassie's gravestone

Mountain View Cemetery chapel

The grounds of Mountain View Cemetery where Cassie is interred

The appeal process of Torey Adamcik

At appeal, Adamcik sought a reduction in the severity of the sentence passed down by retired Sixth District Judge Peter McDermott: life without parole. Boise attorney, Dennis Benjamin, argued that this sentence, imposed on a minor, characterises cruel and unusual punishment.

The
Guilty Innocent

Shannon Adamcik

Shannon Adamcik, mother of Torey, attained a social work degree in the wake of her son's crime, and wrote _The Guilty Innocent._ She may have thought her mothering skills left a lot to be desired. In her book, she laments the Mormon Church's excommunication of Torey. But Mormon murders are all too common. The moment that one of their flock is proclaimed guilty of some horrific crime, they distance themselves, but by then it is far too late. The repressive, hypocritical cult with a blood thirsty history at its source, is in itself a breeding ground for criminal behaviour.

Brian Lee Draper's story as related from the site Mormon Teen World.

I have fixed up only the spelling mistakes for the benefit of the reader. These words of Brian's below were written some years ago, when he was 17, before he was transferred to the adult prison he now resides in. This spiel, written within the first months of his incarceration in a juvenile prison, shows the state of Brian's mind. It is just so much gobbledy gook, an endless diatribe of platitudes mouthed, lacking moral and ethical guidelines: exactly what led him to become the murderer he did become. Pre-marital sex, swearing, and smoking have nothing at all to do with stabbing a young girl to death. They are not the kinds of things that would lead him inexorably down the path to moral degeneration. The consumption of alcohol and drugs are dubious blameworthy agents, as it would depend on how much and what kind were consumed.

His ridiculous argument that "atheism" caused him to become a murderer and that "anarchists" led him astray shows a total lack of understanding of what exactly did take place in his disordered and disturbed mind. The world is full of atheists who lead moral lives and have never as much as harmed a fly, so that argument is out the window for a start.

Ted Bundy serial killer, one of Brian's and Torey's Mormon idols, was an extreme right wing Republican, who used to beat up Liberal left-wing anti-Vietnam demonstrators with a baseball bat. So what, exactly, does he mean by "anarchists"? An anarchist is a person who lives by nobody's rules but his own, and Ted Bundy was certainly one of those. He thinks society's rules do not apply to him, that society has no business setting rules at all; and of course, that fits right in with the psychopathic/sociopathic mind set. A very convenient stance to take.

Sociopaths rationalize their crimes, justifying everything they do: to themselves. We, the general public, who become their hapless victims, are not convinced or taken in by their self-righteous claims. Not all Mormons are heinous murderers either, but the number is growing day by day, and it is particularly evident among the youth of the cult. Historically, Mormon murder was rampant, an everyday occurrence. Metaphorically speaking at least, it's stamped into the Mormon DNA.

Bundy was also an ethical relativist, a great position to take if you want to justify your actions as a serial killer. He thought his desire to bash, rape, kill and commit necrophilia upon female children and young women really had an equal place in the scheme of things with the normal, everyday actions of the rest of us; that we had no right to condemn or judge his "difference" and his chosen way of life. In Bundy's world, our morals held equal status to his lack of them. We were the ones at fault for our inability to accept him as he was. He had a birthright to be a serial killer, or so he thought. He may have realized there was a flaw in his reasoning as he walked, shackled and with shaven head, to the electric chair.

Of course, he was also fully cognizant of the fact that we would bloody well lock him up if we caught him at it, so he kept his ideas and beliefs tightly under wraps; conducting a brilliant charade aimed at preventing us from finding out the truth about his gruesome, disgusting, nocturnal vampirish activities. Though his acting skills could have earned him an Academy Award, his disguise, far from being superlative as he thought, was actually paper thin. It was those closest to him who astutely penetrated the mask: four of them dobbed him in to the cops.

It is things like cruelty metred out to the child, in the form of sexual abuse and physical violence that have been proven to create monsters who kill. The more long term the child is forced to endure it, the greater the damage that is done to the psyche. Yet Bundy refused to tell the world this had happened to him as a boy. It transpired long after Bundy was gone, that sexual abuse by his scout master definitely did occur. This was testified to as fact by the daughter of the abuser.

Similarly, I don't believe for one moment that the families of Torey and Brian are not au fait with the reasons their children were so troubled and violently deranged. They may have been warned in some way of this impending crime. They could have seen the signs and just chosen to ignore them. Were they Jock Mormons, hypocrites into the bargain?

It reminds me of that old song, "He's a youngster, full of fun and we're proud to call him son!" by Harlan Howard, who used to say that all you needed for a great country song was three chords and the truth.

Harlan Howard

He's an all American boy, Mama's pride and Papa's joy
Paper waddin' all the girls, tyin' knots in sister's curls
BB gunnin' passers by with a twinkle in his eye
He's a youngster full of fun and we're proud to call him son
He pushed Grandma down the stairs
then he knelt and said his prayers
And he blessed us one and all and set fire to the hall
While the fireman fought the fire our boy punctured all their tires
He's a youngster full of fun and we're proud to call him son
We went fishin' me and him and he knew I couldn't swim
So this playful little lad tried to drown his lovin' Dad
Nearly caught my death of cold but his mother said "Don't scold!"
He's a youngster full of fun and we're proud to call him son
Well he poisoned Grandma's tea now she lies in agony
Made his mother kind of vexed she says "What will he do next?"

When he shot the neighbor's goats we agreed that's just wild oats
He's a youngster full of fun and we're proud to call him son
Now they took our boy away and we miss him more each day
For our life's adored and tame since the paddy wagon came
We sit and stare in vain through each broken window pane
He's a youngster full of fun and we're proud to call him son

Quote from the Mormon Teen World site

Quote: At 16 he committed murder on a friend, on purpose. He grew up strong in the LDS church and fell away. He is now living forever in fear in a cement box because of the mistakes he made. This is what he has to say. He really is real. You can look up his story of how he planned the murder of a girl to record for a horror movie. And it wasn't till after it was done he had all this to say. Take the time to read this and NOT make the mistakes he made.

My name is Brian Lee Draper and I am in inmate at the Bannock County Jail. I am 17 years old today, but I was just 16 when I was arrested and charged with crimes too heinous to speak of. My purpose in writing this is to tell you of the mistakes that I made in my life which lead me to the life I live today. I write this for those of you who are questioning your faith, or have questioned your faith in the past. Or for those of you, who have gained an unbreakable faith, let this be a reminder to you, to keep living the way you are living, and to never forget what you believe in.

Temptations arise from every direction in your life: drugs, alcohol, stealing, smoking, sexual activities, etc. It is up to you how you handle them; you can give in to them, like I have done, or you can stand strong and stay true to yourself by walking away from them. High school in particular is a time in your life when temptation will confront you continuously. That is what brings me to the topic of friendship. If you choose friends who involve themselves in harmful activities, you will be more susceptible to temptation. No matter how strong you are, when you surround yourself with the wrong people for long enough time, your morals and values which the church have given you crumble and wean away, and you will eventually yield to the temptation, once that occurs you will be more prone to involving yourself in harmful activities.

All throughout my life until I reached the ninth grade, I was an active member in the church, and my heart and soul were filled with God's love. I never thought about the dark side of life. I was never interested in doing things which I knew were wrong. My life was going wonderfully. But when I entered my first year of high school I made a mistake which ended up being the catalyst of my downfall. I chose the wrong friends, and I surrounded myself with them for far too long a time.

When I first met them I knew that these types of people were not the type of people I should be hanging around with, they were atheist: they were anarchist, they were full of negativity. They would tempt me with drugs and alcohol, with cigarettes and larceny. I never gave in, but as the weeks and months went by I was becoming one of them. I surrounded myself with the things they did, and the lifestyles they lived for so long that they now no longer seemed like bad things. Eventually, I gave in to their beliefs and to their lifestyle. I was now living a rebellious lifestyle full of sin and absent of Christ, and I was loving it.

It was so much easier to live this way. I no longer had to fight temptation, and I no longer had to worry about sin because sin didn't exist because God didn't exist. Because of this mentality, my life had no meaning. By the beginning of my junior year I was smoking, going through cars, and my vocabulary was infected with swear words, not only that, but my belief in God was extremely diminished. This drastic turn around in my life all started with the friends I chose. That is why I cannot stress the fact to you enough how important it is to chose good friends. Choose friends with the same morals, and values as you, and they will help you rise up to your full potential. Friends can help you or friends can hurt you. Friends can lift you up, or drag you down.

I know what you are going through because I have been there, and I have made those mistakes. That is why I am writing this. To tell you to keep as far away from the bad things in life, and know what they are. Never let go, or even lighten your grip on the iron rod. Letting go will lead you to nothing but pain. You will be lost, and you will have to find your way back. But if you never let go you will never lose yourself. God will show you who you are because when you have Christ in your life and in your heart, all of your beauty will shine, and you will be the best person that you are capable of being. High school and teenage years are extremely tough years, but they will pass, and you will thank God that you never gave in to the temptation. Your youth is a small part of your life, so hold out until the end.

Life will not necessarily get much easier after your teenage years have passed, but you will be matured, and your faith will be matured. You will be successful if you live a life in Christ. He will give you nothing that you can't handle. You can ruin your life and your future by the mistakes that you make in your youth. I have had to learn that lesson the hard way. I turned my back on my heavenly father, and every night while I sit on a metal bed in a concrete cell, I wish I hadn't. If I would have had God in my life I can say honestly I would not be in the situation I am in. So many of my elders tried to tell me that the way I was living was wrong, but I would always ignore their friendly advice. In my mind what I was doing wasn't wrong. I was just being a teenager. Nothing would happen to me.

When my best friend from school comes to visit me at the jail, I look into his eyes and see the old me. I see everything that I once was. I see such foolishness, such naiveté. I now realize how stupid I was to be atheist. I was stupid for living the way I was. My friend's beginning to use drugs and drink alcohol. He is failing school and is in jeopardy of not graduating. He still caries all the same beliefs which I used to carry, and his life is going nowhere, because he has denied Christ, and is still surrounding himself with desolate people. So many teens are living as my friend is living, not realizing what the lifestyle will lead to - a life on the street, prison, or dead.

I know from firsthand experience that nothing that Satan has put here on this earth has the ability to impact our life in a positive way. Living a life absent Christ seems enjoyable at first, but it will lead you to nothing but pain and sorrow. Remember; it all starts small. Small sins will lead to larger sins. Think of a snowball rolling down a hill. The snowball represents you life, the snow is sin. As the snowball rolls down the hill more and more is added upon it. It gets larger and larger until it reaches the bottom of the hill and smashes to pieces. If you begin sinning here and there- off and on- the sins will start adding up. And growing. When you are full of sin you will reach the bottom, and your world will crumble.

Many youth today think of going to church and studying scriptures as a chore. You should be fervent in your scripture study. You should have a desire to learn more and more about your father in heaven, and in the gospel. Church, the scriptures, prayer, church activities; these are all tools to help you live a better life.

Some of you might think the church has too many rules. These are not rules, not participating in drugs or alcohol, keeping the Sabbath day holy, dressing appropriate, not lying, cheating, stealing, or swearing, not engaging in premarital sex; all of these subjects of advice. The church and the Lord have created these subjects of advice to help you live a better life, and to rise up to your full potential. None of these things can help you in attaining your maximum potential. That is why God and the church have asked you not to do them. It was Fulton J. Sheen who wrote: "Our Lord did not ask us to give up the things of Earth, but to exchange them for better things".

Remember mortality is but a small part of our existence. Your life on this earth is a test, a test to see if you are worthy of someday again living with your heavenly father. So live each day with the fullness of the Lord and his gospel within your heart. When temptations arise strike them down. Your heavenly father will always be there for you. He will never leave you, so never leave him.

There is a little poem I found in a book entitled; "Where Eagles Rest". It goes as follows: "There is no chance, no destiny, no fate, that can circumvent, or hinder, or control the firm resolve of a determined soul". So with this statement, be determined to be the best, most righteous person you can be. Be determined to rise up to your full potential, and live a life of Christ, so you may someday live with him again. Do not allow evil to hinder your plan to reach heaven. Evil knocked at the door; faith answered; no one was there.

I wish you all the best of luck in life. Please do not make the same mistakes I have made, and please "Look not at the things which are seen, but at the things which are not seen: for the things which are seen are temporal: but the things which are not seen are eternal. (Corinthians 24:18)

With nothing but love and sincerity,
Your friend, Brian Lee Draper inmate:148332. End Quote.

Family rallies for excommunicated Mormon Torey

Family members pulled out all stoppers during the appeals process for Torey Adamcik, leaving no stone unturned, even convincing Torey's teacher from Middle School to come to his aid. They entreated her to testify alongside them as to Torey's character, which she did. Rusty Adamson from Hawthorne Middle School, said she knew Torey to be immature, and a follower, not a leader. "He had friends, but he was willing to hang back and let them take the lead," Adamson said.

Hawthorne Middle School, which Torey attended

But Ms Adamson had not been teaching Torey in his years immediately prior to the murder conviction, and had no recent knowledge of his character development. When Service asked Adamson if she had taught Torey Adamcik between seventh and

44

tenth grade, Adamson admitted she had not. But she said Torey Adamcik came back to middle school to visit her on occasion.

Torey during his appeals process

The Pocatello defense team of Aaron Thompson, Greg May and Bron Rammell, represented Torey Adamcik in his 2007 murder trial. They originally planned to call character witnesses on his behalf in an attempt to distinguish him from co-defendant, Brian Draper.

But this plan was thrown into a cocked hat when Bannock County Prosecutor Mark Heideman advised Thompson he intended to present to the court a disc downloaded from a computer in the Adamcik family room. The disc contained child pornography, evidence of cruelty to animals and images from horror movies. Thompson said the prosecutor told him that if the defense team dropped the character defense, they would not present the disc.

Who downloaded the child pornography, the images of cruelty to animals in the Adamcik home – father Sean or son Torey?

"We were very worried about that information coming in," Thompson said. "Our strategy kind of shifted." Boise attorney Dennis Benjamin, who specializes in appeals and post-conviction proceedings, represented Torey Adamcik. Benjamin argued that Adamcik should be granted a new trial, or at least a new sentencing for his role in the murder of Cassie Jo Stoddart. Benjamin asked Thompson if motions had been filed to suppress or exclude the images from the computer, and Thompson said no motion was filed. Thompson said no motion was filed regarding the search of the Adamcik residence, which netted the disc. "If I had thought that there was any legal basis to file a motion, I would have," Thompson said.

Torey Adamcik's father, Sean Adamcik, said the family was called to the law library of May, Rammell and Thompson when the disc was discovered. He said he watched a few frames, ejected the disc and observed that it had been created about six weeks earlier. He then argued that the timing of the discovery rendered the disc invalid as a weapon for the prosecution to use against Torey and aid in his conviction. "I looked at it and I told them they didn't just get this (recently)," Sean said. "I told them that it had to be a late discovery and the images didn't have anything to do with the charges against Torey."

Bannock County Deputy Prosecutor Ian Service asked Sean Adamick if it was his opinion that the images in the disc were not child pornography, and if he recalled seeing images of animal skulls and skeletons in disarray, an image of a Rambo-type knife or a pentagon carved into bloody flesh. Sean Adamcik skirted this question, saying he remembered seeing only movie and CD jackets. Benjamin noted that the boys in the pornographic images contained on the disc were about the same age as Torey Adamcik was in 2006.

Thompson said he did file a motion to suppress a police interview with Torey Adamcik. During the interview, Torey Adamcik said he thought he should have his attorney present. But officers continued to talk to his father, and at one point, Torey Adamcik nodded his head. Judge Peter McDermott excluded part of the interview.

A mother's torment and the plea for her son to be released from prison one day

Louise Bundy was Ted's staunchest ally, even after he made his confession, just hours before his Raiford Prison execution. Even then, she valiantly and in true maternal style, told him he would always be her precious son. Mothers are notoriously unreliable in their estimation of their sons' worth to the world. Torey Adamcik's mother, Shannon, took the stand and told the court the character defense was "half" of their case. "I wanted the jury to know him, to know Torey and the difference between him and Draper," Shannon Adamcik said. "This was not the defense we expected."

Shannon also testified that at one point, the prosecution said if Torey pleaded guilty, they would not make any sentencing recommendations in the murder case. "But the judge could have still sentenced him to life without parole," she said. No other plea deals were presented to them. Torey Adamcik, now 25, made notes and watched the court proceedings of the appeal closely.

Torey Adamcik's sister, Lacey, said she drove her brother to school every day and the family had dinner together every night. "Torey loved movies, music and drawing," Lacey said. "He was friendly. He always had a lot of friends at the house."

Service objected to putting the character witnesses on the stand, but Benjamin argued that it demonstrated how the character defense might have affected the case. Torey Adamcik was transported to Bannock County from Boise for the appeal to be heard.

About a dozen of Cassie Jo Stoddart's family members were in the courtroom. Her grandfather, Paul Cisneros, said he has had no contact with the Adamcik family since his granddaughter Cassie was murdered.

Brian Draper's appeal and his mother's pain
In Boise, the lawyer for Brian Draper, convicted of killing his high school classmate Cassie Jo Stoddart nearly five years before the appeal was heard; asked Idaho Supreme Court justices to dump his conviction or reduce his sentence.

State appellate public defender Molly Huskey told justices that sentencing Brian Draper, who was 16 at the time of the crime, to life in prison without the possibility of parole would be unconstitutionally cruel.

Huskey argued a district court judge erred in sentencing Draper to the fixed life term. Huskey said her client's immaturity and poor judgment were partially attributable to his youth at the time of the crime and that he deserved a chance for release. She also said the jury received erroneous instructions. "Even if this court finds that a fixed life sentence can be imposed on a juvenile, that sentence cannot be imposed based solely on the egregiousness of the offense," Huskey said. If justices won't vacate his conviction, she argued they should give him a life sentence that allows for his release after 30 years.

Brian Draper has admitted his guilt and proclaims remorse for the killing of Cassie Jo Stoddart. His entire life will be spent behind bars unless at some time in the future his appeal is upheld. Brian's parents have stated that they did not recognize Brian's problems and if they had, they would have sought clinical help for him. They adopted Brian when he was a small child and say they "had a great relationship with him" before the crime.

Idaho State Deputy Attorney General John McKinney urged the State High Court to uphold the ruling. McKinney cited Draper and Adamcik's video, which showed their excitement immediately following the slaying where Stoddart was stabbed more than 30 times in the house where she was pet-sitting for family members.

That recording, McKinney said, showed how Draper turned on Stoddart only to experience taking another person's life — even if it happened to be the life of a friend. "It doesn't get any worse than that," McKinney said. "He did it for the thrill of killing somebody."

Pamela Draper, Brian's mother, told The Associated Press through tears, "We're just holding it together." Following the hearing, Brian's parents waited to speak to Cassie's family. "Every time we see you, we just feel terrible," an emotional Kerry Draper told Anna Stoddart. "I know it's our son, and we still feel the need to support him. But we just feel terrible."

Before the hearing, Cassie Jo Stoddart's mother, Anna, and grandfather Paul Cisneros described the pain of losing a child and grandchild to violent crime. "We've come to watch what happens — and to show we care," her grandfather said. The Idaho Supreme Court upheld the convictions of both Draper and Adamcik.

Cycle Cassie Jo Stoddart was undergoing at the time of her death.

Every year, our Numerological Personal Year is divided up into 3, four-month cycles.

The first of these runs from our birthday until 4 months hence, and that one is ruled by the age we are at the time.

The second of these cycles is ruled by our Life Lesson Number, the date on which we were born.

The third of these cycles is ruled by our Soul Numbers, that is, the value of the vowels in our name.

The time of day which decrees when we emerge out of one particular (numerically designated) Personal Year, Cycle, Month or Day and enter the next, equates with the time of day at which we were born.

Notice that Cassie was born on the 21st, and she was killed on the 22nd. Brian Draper's and Torey Adamcik's voices as recorded on videotape say they have killed Cassie Jo Stoddart at 11.32pm on the 22nd. However, the videotaping of Cassie began on the morning of the 22nd, and this was all part of the plan to kill Cassie. The murder was already in progress, you might say. At that point in time, her life was in mortal danger. The first recording we have of Cassie taken by her killer/s, was on the morning of her death, when she was loading her school books into her locker before the start of the school day, around 8.30am. She does not know it, but her life then was almost over. That fact is known only to her interviewer, one of her intending killers, Brian Draper, who is speaking to her as cool as a cucumber, in a friendly, affable manner. Corey Adamcik had not yet arrived at school, according to Draper.

Draper here reminds me very much of Ted Bundy chatting away to his victim as he led her to her death, while she carried his books for him out of kindness; poor injured fellow student with his arm or leg in a plaster cast, that he pretended to be. Draper has learnt his serial killer lessons well. It was thought by some that Bundy chose his victims at random. That is true, he did on many occasions; but on many others we have evidence that he was stalking particular girls and women for quite some time before he pounced.

He knew 8 year old Ann Marie Burr from his paper route; she thought this handsome older 14 year old boy her hero. A neighbour said little Ann would have gone anywhere with him if he had asked. She was abducted from her bedroom one night and her body never found.

Margaret Bowman was Bundy's main target when he entered the Chi Omega vestibule, and he could see at a glance which room she was in. Up on the wall, all the names of the girls were marked beside the location and number of the room they occupied. It is thought he checked this out earlier in the day, because the sorority house cat was spooked and ran away that day; hours before the murders were committed; and did not return for a fortnight.

Another of Bundy's university victims, Lynda Ann Healy, a psychology student like himself, was known to him through Jane, his first cousin on the Cowell side of the family, with whom he had grown up. Jane had met Lynda, but she could not recall if Ted had; though she said they attended the same parties together.

In like manner; I have reason to believe Cassie was chosen by Brian Draper and Corey Adamcik long before that video was recorded; in fact, I believe she was chosen long before the month of September, and here is the reason why I do believe that.

Here is the 4-month Cycle Cassie was undergoing **between 21st April and 21st August, 2006**, ruled by her Life Lesson Number of 60/6. (21st December, 1989 = 21+12+27=60/6)

2005 year of last birthday
   60 + Life Lesson Number
2065**= **13/4** Cycle, mediated through the **Master 65/11**

Roman Numerals XIII = 13th card Death in the Tarot Deck.
Master 65 = King of Pentacles in the Tarot Deck.
Roman Numerals XI = Master 11 Justice card in the Tarot Deck

In interpreting these numbers and corresponding symbolic cards in relation to what has transpired, namely, the murder of Cassie, I am going to be referring only to the possible negative manifestations of these cards. The King of Pentacles/Master 65 is predominantly ruled by Capricorn. Cassie was born on the 21st of December, right on the cusp of Sagittarius/Capricorn. The people born on this cusp, roughly a few days either side of the 21st of December, are sometimes jokingly referred to as Sagicorns, and thought to have the gift of prophecy. Their symbol is of course, the mythical unicorn. They are said to be among those who will lead the world.

However, this card does have connections with signs other than Capricorn. Note the 4 symbols of the bull on the throne. There is a connection with the sign of Taurus the bull, but also Gemini, according to the ancient texts. Torey is a Geminian. Negatively expressed, this card can bring a tendency towards possessiveness with friends and lovers, and controlling behaviour.

The combination of this card with the Death Card and the Justice Card which rules the law courts and criminal prosecution, symbolizes what was to be the dreadful outcome of this combination of negative traits expressed in the direction of Cassie Jo Stoddart. Brian has since said that he and Torey together were a "formula for disaster" and these cards do suggest that.

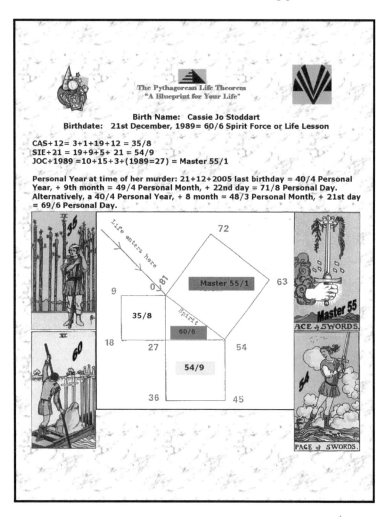

The Pythagorean Life Theorem
"A Blueprint for Your Life"

Birth Name: Cassie Jo Stoddart
Birthdate: 21st December, 1989= 60/6 Spirit Force or Life Lesson

CAS+12= 3+1+19+12 = 35/8
SIE+21 = 19+9+5+ 21 = 54/9
JOC+1989 =10+15+3+(1989=27) = Master 55/1

Personal Year at time of her murder: 21+12+2005 last birthday = 40/4 Personal Year, + 9th month = 49/4 Personal Month, + 22nd day = 71/8 Personal Day. Alternatively, a 40/4 Personal Year, + 8 month = 48/3 Personal Month, + 21st day = 69/6 Personal Day.

When Cassie was murdered, she had progressed out of her second cycle and into her third, the one ruled by her **Soul Numbers**. This Personal Cycle for Cassie ran from **21st August to 21st December, 2006** and was ruled by her **Soul Numbers** of 28 and the Master 22.

2005 last birthday
  28+
20 33 = 8

2005
  22+
20 27 = Master 11/2

So, at the time of her death, Cassie was passing through a combination Master 11 and 8 Cycle, mediated through the Number 27/9 and the Master 33/6.

22 Sept 2006	1:06 pm	The Moon entered Libra which equates with the Justice Card and the Master Number 11

Calendar for September 2006 (United States)

September

Sun	Mon	Tue	Wed	Thu	Fri	Sat
					1	2
3	4	5	6	7	8	9
10	11	12	13	14	15	16
17	18	19	20	21	22	23
24	25	26	27	28	29	30

Phases of the moon: 7: 14: 22: 30:
Holidays and Observances: 4: Labor Day   New Moon: 22nd

In looking at the Moon cycles for September 2006 - notice how dark the sky would have been on the night Cassie was murdered the 22nd. When Brian and Torey turned off the electricity the house would have been in total darkness, very frightening for her indeed. But this was only a prelude to the real terror that was awaiting her.

An annular solar eclipse occurred on September 22, 2006. A solar eclipse occurs when the Moon passes between Earth and the Sun, thereby totally or partly obscuring the image of the Sun for a viewer on Earth. An annular solar eclipse occurs when the Moon's apparent diameter is smaller than the Sun's, blocking most of the Sun's light and causing the Sun to look like an annulus or ring. An annular eclipse appears as a partial eclipse over a region of the Earth thousands of kilometres wide.

Common sense dictates that since the moon rules the tides of the oceans and the menstrual cycle of females both animal and human, the ebb and flow of life on earth, that something significant like an annular solar eclipse would have an affect on human behaviour. This knowledge and understanding is accepted in a great many cultures around the world, where scientific research has been conducted to verify the truth of something humans have always known from their thousands of years of empirical observation, which is, in and of itself, a scientific study.

Here is a report of a controlled scientific study conducted in 2011, showing the effect of solar eclipse on life at the microbic level. This study was conducted 4 years ago, yet still we have western scientists trying to tell us that the effect of eclipses on earthly behaviour is "superstition".

This is the dictionary definition of what superstition is considered to be:-
(a) a belief or notion, not based on reason or knowledge, in or of the ominous significance of a particular thing, circumstance, occurrence, proceeding, or the like
(b) a system or collection such beliefs
(c) a custom or act based on such a belief
(d) irrational fear of what is unknown or mysterious, especially in connection with religion

(e) any blindly accepted belief or notion

Yet notice the era this word was coined and introduced into the English language. The dictionary says the word "superstition" was first used between 1375 and 1425, and is of Late Middle English origin. But what was happening at that time in history, in that part of the world? Its use is first recorded in writing c1420 in Friar Daw's Reply, when the hanging of friars was the order of the day. He castigates his detractors as not knowing "A from a windmill or B from a bull's foot." Gee, just shows you how old that saying is too!

Simultaneously, it is recorded that between 1300 and 1350 the word "persecution" was introduced into the Middle English language, meaning to follow, pursue, as in the pursuit of or chase; persecution means literally, "the hunt to bring someone down like an animal," trying to suppress and punish them for their beliefs and convictions.

So, what does that tell us? The suppression of those beliefs which are still, even now in 2015, derisively called superstitions originally occurred as the result of religious and cultural persecution during the Late Middle Ages. To be a heretic meant your life would be taken. Heresy was a treasonable crime. Religion, scientific thought, the nature and direction of research and inquiry was decreed by the King, his preferred religion and most importantly of all, those who wielded the most power; the church hierarchy.

So much valuable knowledge was suppressed, so many thousands of scholars and intellectuals, not to mention autodidactically educated lay people, were horrifically tortured to death or murdered in cold blood during that era, that we have not even yet, climbed out of the mire of terror to rediscover what was common knowledge to them. The baby was thrown out with the bath water in willy nilly fashion. Fear and reluctance to discover by moving in forbidden directions of inquiry is still endemic among the populace, and nowhere is it more prevalent than in our western institutions and universities.

The Pythagorean Life Theorem
"A Blueprint for Your Life"

Birth Name: Brian Lee Draper
Birthdate: 21st March, 1990= 43/7 Spirit Force or Life Lesson

BRI +3 = 2+18+9+3 = 32/5
ANL+21 = 1+14+12+21 = 48/3
EEB+1990 = 5+5+2+19 = 31/4

Personal Year at time of Cassie Jo Stoddart's murder: 21+3+2006
last birthday = 32/5 Personal Year, + 9th month = (32+9)= 41/5
Personal Month, + 22nd day = (41+22) = 63/9 Personal Day

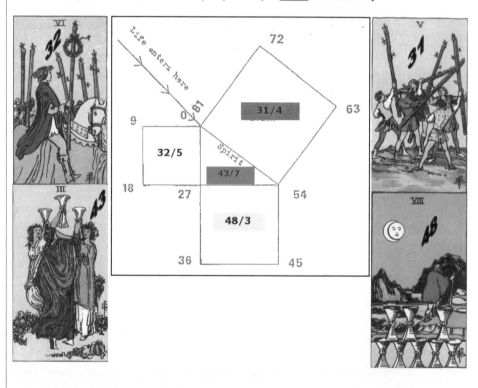

Notice the eclipse symbol on the chart of Brian Draper. Could Brian's behaviour have been affected by his eclipse?

While humans have always perceived eclipses to coincide with disastrous events, so too did they understand that the phases of the sun and moon were vital to sustaining life on earth. The timing of the planting and harvesting of crops were known to be best done in cooperation and harmony with the sun, moon and stars, and not in antipathy with them. Not only were disastrous events connected with the movement of the celestial bodies, so too were all the wonders of nature aided and abetted by them in their nourishment and growth. Healthy, luxuriant crops were vital to a healthy populace.

Modern scientific experiments, conducted under controlled conditions in laboratories, at least in the east, seems to be moving in the direction of an understanding of how we can harness the power of the eclipse to eradicate disease and aid humankind. Hopefully, these small steps will one day lead to a greater understanding of the effect the eclipse can have on human behaviour.

The study below found that "blocking of the sun rays during eclipse does not harm prokaryotes and eukaryotes, instead **promoted the progeny of predators** in the race of better acclimatization and survival **in the natural and changing environmental conditions**."

If eclipses stimulate predators at the cellular level, might they also, in some as yet unknown way, kick start deviant or violently aggressive behaviour in those human beings who already have exhibited the potential for same? Might they serve as accelerants to the spark, igniting it into flame? Would those among us with predatory instincts be somehow stimulated at the time of eclipses? Our human brains are after all, physical organs within our flesh and blood bodies. At the cellular level, we are not unlike the subjects used in the following experiment.

Effect of solar eclipse on microbes

Amrita Shriyan, Angri M. Bhat, and Narendra Nayak
http://www.ncbi.nlm.nih.gov/pmc/articles/PMC3053514/

Objective: A solar eclipse was observed in India on 15th January, 2010. It was a total eclipse in some parts of the country, while it was a partial eclipse in other parts. Microorganisms play an important role in various phenomena on the earth. This study was undertaken to know the influence of solar eclipse on nature indirectly, by analyzing certain genotypic and phenotypic variations in prokaryotes and eukaryotes. Since yeast have similar gene expression as that of humans, investigations were pursued on Candida albicans. Hence the study of the effect of solar eclipse on cultures of Staphylococcus aureus, Klebsiella species, Escherichia coli, and C. albicans was performed in the laboratory. The effect of the total or partial eclipse on the microorganism isolated from clinical isolates was investigated during the time period from 11.15 am to 3.15 pm.

Results and Conclusion
There was significant change observed during exposure to normal sunlight and eclipse phase. Bacterial colonies showed difference in morphology on smear examination and sensitivity pattern during this study. One fungal species and three bacterial isolates were studied and changes were recorded. Fungal species showed a definite change in their morphology on exposure to sunlight during eclipse observed by stained smear examination from broth, plate, and slant.

Present study concludes that blocking of the sun rays during eclipse does not harm prokaryotes and eukaryotes, instead promoted the progeny of predators in the race of better acclimatization and survival in the natural and changing environmental conditions.

Our observations have important implications of solar eclipse and their induced variations. To our knowledge, such studies have not been reported previously for S. aureus, Klebsiellaspecies, E. coli, and C. albicans in clinical isolates. However from our studies, we could infer that exposure to solar eclipse does help in the favor of microbes and man. Further study is needed in this area to use solar eclipse therapeutically to enhance the immune system and targeting the destruction of genesis of malignant cells thus, to alleviate the suffering of humankind. End of Quote.

From my numerological analysis, I feel that Torey Adamcik was probably the dominant partner, or at the very least, equally culpable in this horrific crime. However, I do not know whether Brian's birth parents may have given him a name prior to the one he currently now owns, i.e. the one given to him by his adoptive parents.

My Numerological System

A = 1	J = 10/1	S = 19/1
B = 2	K = 11/2	T = 20/2
C = 3	L = 12/3	U = 21/3
D = 4	M = 13/4	V = 22/4
E = 5	N = 14/5	W = 23/5
F = 6	O = 15/6	X = 24/6
G = 7	P = 16/7	Y = 25/7

Each letter takes its value from its place in the alphabet. For example, the letter "P" as the 16th letter of the alphabet, has the value 16. This in turn can be reduced down to 7. (16 = 1+6 =7). So, it is written 16/7.

55/10/1
11/2
66/12/3
22/4
77/14/5
33/6
88/16/7
44/8
99/18/9

29/11
38/11
47/11
56/11
65/11
74/11
83/11
92/11

The Master Numbers are 11, any multiple of 11, and any number that reduces to 11. They represent the highest elevation of the base digits, 1 to 9. All those numbers which reduce to **11**, are variations and different aspects or manifestations of the **Master 11,** which equates with the **Justice Card**. As such, it rules the Law Courts.

The basic tools of my numerological system

The numbers and their and Tarot correspondence I use in my forensic numerological criminal profiling:-

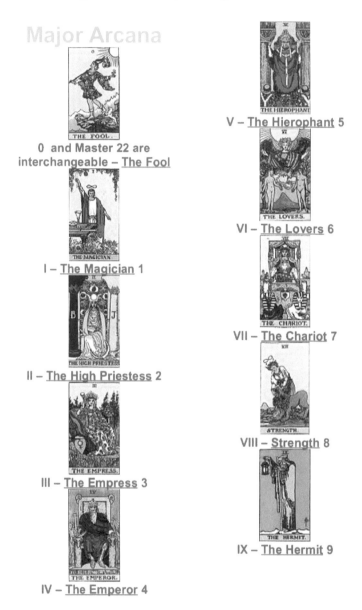

Major Arcana

0 and Master 22 are interchangeable – The Fool

I – The Magician 1

II – The High Priestess 2

III – The Empress 3

IV – The Emperor 4

V – The Hierophant 5

VI – The Lovers 6

VII – The Chariot 7

VIII – Strength 8

IX – The Hermit 9

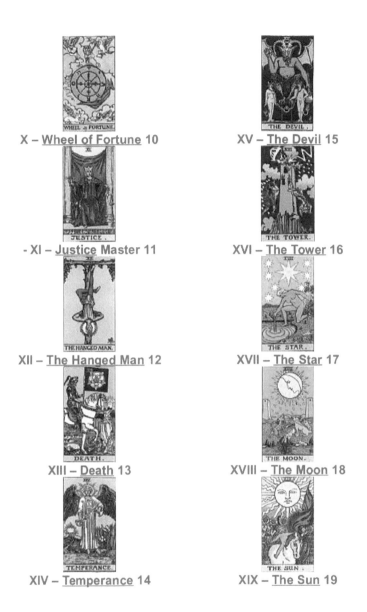

X – Wheel of Fortune 10

XV – The Devil 15

- XI – Justice Master 11

XVI – The Tower 16

XII – The Hanged Man 12

XVII – The Star 17

XIII – Death 13

XVIII – The Moon 18

XIV – Temperance 14

XIX – The Sun 19

XX – Judgement 20

Three of Wands Master 29

XXI – The World 21

Four of Wands 30

The Fool Master 22

Five of Wands 31

Wands

Six of Wands 32

Ace of Wands 27

Seven of Wands Master 33

Two of Wands 28

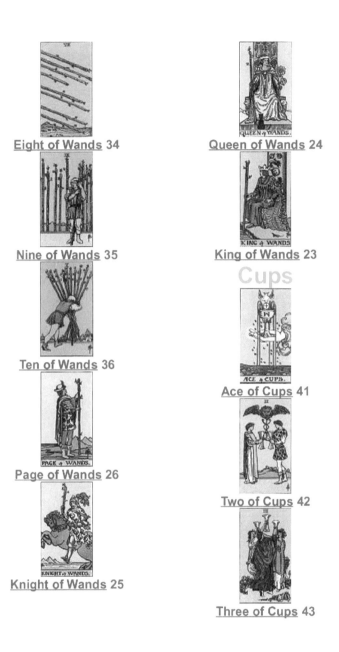

Eight of Wands 34

Queen of Wands 24

Nine of Wands 35

King of Wands 23

Cups

Ten of Wands 36

Ace of Cups 41

Page of Wands 26

Two of Cups 42

Knight of Wands 25

Three of Cups 43

Four of Cups Master 44　　　　Nine of Cups 49

Five of Cups 45　　　　Ten of Cups 50

Six of Cups 46　　　　Page of Cups 40

Seven of Cups Master 47　　　　Knight of Cups 39

Eight of Cups 48　　　　Queen of Cups Master 38

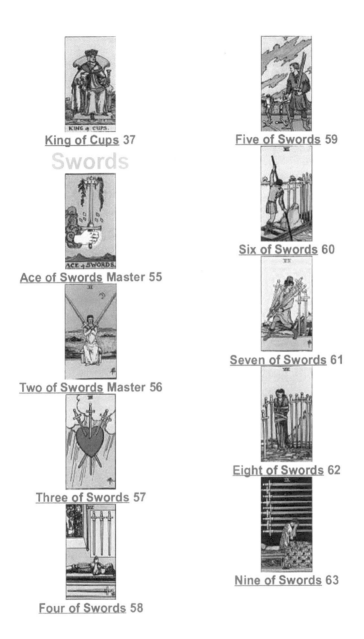

King of Cups 37

Swords

Ace of Swords Master 55

Two of Swords Master 56

Three of Swords 57

Four of Swords 58

Five of Swords 59

Six of Swords 60

Seven of Swords 61

Eight of Swords 62

Nine of Swords 63

Ten of Swords 64

Page of Swords 54

Knight of Swords 53

Queen of Swords 52

King of Swords 51

Ace of Pentacles 69

Two of Pentacles 70

Three of Pentacles 71

Four of Pentacles 72

Five of Pentacles 73

Pentacles

Six of Pentacles Master 74

Seven of Pentacles 75

Eight of Pentacles 76

Nine of Pentacles Master 77

Ten of Pentacles 78

Page of Pentacles 68

Knight of Pentacles 67

Queen of Pentacles Master 66

King of Pentacles Master 65

Suffering of the perpetrators' families

The lives that get torn apart when a tragedy such as this strikes, do not only belong to the victim. Rarely does the same kind of sympathy extend to the families of the perpetrators of the crime. I have expressed my opinion about the Mormon religion, and how I believe it is not conducive to raising well-adjusted children, particularly boys. The repressiveness of it seems to breed rebellion not of the normal variety we come to expect with teenagers. It does instead tend to breed hypocrisy and deviancy, in that the repression of a normal life for young people is denied them. Here are some family snaps of life lived for the Draper and Adamcik families before, during and after this tragedy struck their lives. There is no mistaking the love and devotion shared, but the happy smiles belie what lies beneath.

The Draper Family

The Adamcik family

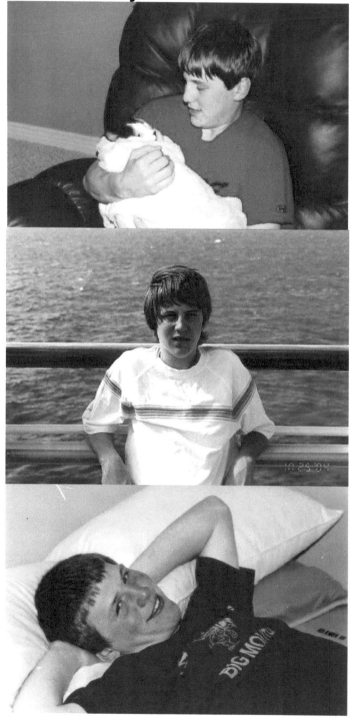

Adamcik:—the point I'm makin' is . . . we are also taught that things like killing people and other things is wrong. The only thing that is wrong about is because it's breaking the law and the law is only wrong (mumbling, searching for words)—

Draper: Natural selection, dude. Natural selection, that's all I've gotta say.

Adamcik: There should be no law against killing people. I know it's a wrong thing, but . . .

Draper: Natural selection—

Adamcik:—Hell, hell, you restrict somebody from it, they're just gonna want it more.

Draper: We'll let you . . . (laughs) we'll find out if she has friends over, if she's going to be alone in a big dark house out in the middle of nowhere (laughs). How perfect can you get? I, I mean like holy shit dude.

Adamcik: I'm horny just thinking about it.

Draper: We're gonna be murderers. Like, let's see, Ted Bundy, like the Hillside Strangler.

Adamcik: No.

Draper: The Zodiac Killer.

Adamcik: Those people were more amateurs compared to what we are going to be, we're gonna be more of higher sources of Ed gl . . .

Draper: Gein

Adamcik: Gein

Adamcik: For you future serial killers watching this tape

Adamcik & Draper: (laughing)

Adamcik: I don't know what to say.

Draper: It-It's—

Adamcik:—good luck with that.

Draper: Good luck.

Adamcik: Hopefully you don't have like 8 or 9 failures like we have.

More evidence against Torey

At trial, the jury heard extensive forensic testimony documenting and analyzing Stoddart's wounds. The medical examiner, Dr. Steve Skoumal, performed the autopsy on Stoddart on September 25th 2006. Dr. Skoumal determined that the cause of Stoddart's death was stab wounds to the trunk. In all, Dr. Skoumal documented thirty knife-related wounds on Stoddart's body, twelve of which were potentially fatal.

The State also had forensic pathologist Dr. Charles Garrison examine Stoddart's body. Dr. Garrison testified "It's my opinion that there were at least two knives used, one of which was a non-serrated blade, and one of which was a serrated blade."

In general, the majority of the potentially fatal wounds that Dr. Skoumal listed were inflicted with the serrated blade, however, wound number 1, which struck the right ventricle of Stoddart's heart, was inflicted by a non-serrated blade—consistent with Dr. Garrison's testimony—and was potentially fatal.

Now, I find this very interesting. I have already stated that I believe Brian in all likelihood delivered a fatal stabbing wound to Cassie's heart, but this evidence states that Torey was in all likelihood the one who delivered a knife thrust to the heart that resulted in Cassie's death. Torey does have on his chart the Number 57/3, the symbolism of which shows three swords piercing a heart, and since he was in the murderous 59/5 Personal Day on the day of the murder, it is very difficult indeed to gauge which one of the youths actually delivered the fatal blow.

We must also bear in mind it is sheer conjecture which youth used which knife at the time of the murder. Just because one boy verbally owned to preferring a certain kind of knife when purchasing it from the supplier, does not necessarily mean that he and he alone used that knife on that night. The knives for both boys were purchased at one and the same time from the same supplier. They were jointly paid for. There were a variety of weapons seized in the wake of the crime. As far as I am aware, it has not been definitely established which boy used which particular knife. Torey's claims to innocence seem to be centred on lack of DNA evidence - pointing to his exclusion from participation. However, in the final (numerological) analysis, I believe both Brian and Torey rained a frenzy of stabbing blows upon the body of their hapless, terrified victim Cassie, and which of the stab wounds was the one that killed her is really not the question we need to be asking in regard to their joint culpability for her resultant agonizing and tragic death.

Lightning Source UK Ltd.
Milton Keynes UK
UKHW052020100223
416857UK00001B/1

* 9 7 8 1 3 2 6 4 1 8 5 2 6 *